W9-ABG-773

BAD GUYS

LEGENDARY

GUNSLINGERS,
SIDEWINDERS,
FOURFLUSHERS,
DRYGULCHERS,
BUSHWHACKERS,
FREEBOOTERS,
AND DOWNRIGHT
BAD GUYS AND GALS
OF THE WILD WEST

ANDREW GLASS

A DOUBLEDAY BOOK FOR YOUNG READERS

A Doubleday Book for Young Readers
Published by
Bantam Doubleday Dell Publishing Group, Inc.
1540 Broadway, New York, New York 10036
Doubleday and the portrayal of an anchor with a dolphin are trademarks of Bantam Doubleday Dell Publishing Group, Inc.

Library of Congress Cataloging-in-Publication Data
Glass, Andrew.
Bad Guys: true stories of legendary gunslingers, sidewinders, fourflushers, drygulchers, bushwhackers, freebooters, and downright bad guys and gals of the Wild West / Andrew Glass.
p. cm.
Summary: Relates the exploits of several famous outlaws in frontier America such as Wild Bill Hickok, Calamity Jane, and Doc Holliday.
ISBN 0-385-32310-7
1. Outlaws—West (U.S.)—Biography—Juvenile literature. 2. West (U.S.)—Biography—Juvenile literature. 3. Frontier and pioneer life—West (U.S.)— Juvenile literature. [1. Robbers and outlaws—West (U.S.) 2. Frontier and pioneer life—West (U.S.) 3. West (U.S.)—History.] I. Title.
F594.G53 1998
364.18558092278—dc21
[B] 97-31408
CIP
AC

The text of this book is set in 14-point Cheltenham Book.
Book design by Trish P. Watts
Manufactured in the United States of America
November 1998
10 9 8 7 6 5 4 3 2 1

I was waiting my turn for a regular boy's haircut in a barbershop that was just a shack along Route 66 near the high school when I picked up a dog-eared copy of the Police Gazette *and read "The True Story of Doc Holliday." I can't remember much else I learned in fourth grade, but I remember well that pulp article about the dentist determined to die with his boots on and how it ignited my imagination. So I dedicate this book to the first time I learned something I really wanted to know by reading.*

—ANDREW GLASS

The Wild

After the Civil War ended, in 1865, most Americans set about rebuilding their nation. Soon hardworking folks in the East began to hear fantastical stories about the untamed West, stories of mysterious drifters and handsome, freewheeling gunfighters shooting it out in dusty cow towns with names like Tombstone, Dodge City, and Abilene. Eastern newspapers printed wildly exaggerated articles about these Western adventurers as if they were fact. And their readers just couldn't get enough.

Real gunslingers weren't looking to set the record straight, either. Many found time between shoot-outs to jot down a few whoppers describing their lightning-fast draw or dead

West

aim with a six-shooter. They figured it was to their advantage to be legends. Legends made folks nervous! Bat Masterson took advantage of his reputation as a fast gun to scare off ordinary tough guys. Actually, he may never have shot anyone when he was sheriff of Dodge City, Kansas, called "the wickedest town on earth." Truth is, Bat figured that shooting cowboys could get him killed. So he preferred to keep the drunks in line by denting their heads with his fancy walking stick. That's how he got his nickname, Bat.

Wild Bill Hickok invented thrilling yarns for wide-eyed Eastern newspapermen. He bragged to Henry M. Stanley (of "Dr. Livingstone, I presume" fame) that he'd killed well over a hundred men, not counting Indians. In fact, he had shot more than a few people, and like most of his fellow gunslingers, Wild Bill was himself finally gunned down.

Clay Allison first elevated gunslinging to a profession, calling himself a "shootist." In popular dime novels, shootists shot it out face-to-face in fair fights. Wild Bill may have risked such duels. There is at least one on record. But shootists preferred to "get the drop" on their opponents by jumping out at them from dark alleyways, squeezing off a shot from behind a curtain, or simply shooting them in the back.

Shootists came from all over. Billy the Kid was born in a New York slum. Frank and Jesse James were sons of a Missouri preacher and sang in the choir on Sundays. Doc Holliday and Johnny Ringo claimed to be descended from genteel aristocrats, and Dave Mather could trace his family back to the New England witch-hunter Cotton Mather.

Fortune hunters who flocked westward in the 1860s and 1870s were often avoiding arrest or running out on their debts. *GTT* (Gone to Texas) scrawled on the door of an abandoned house let the local sheriff or bill collector know the former occupants had moved on to start a new life. Most worked in mining towns and on farms and cattle ranches. Others sharpened their shooting skills as buffalo hunters in the massacre of the great herds. But some chose easier ways to make a living, such as gambling.

Gambling was the part-time profession of many shootists. Cardsharps fleeced young workers of their wages and bought saloons with their winnings. Wild Bill Hickok, Wyatt Earp, and Bat Masterson were full-time cardsharps and part-time lawmen.

Other trigger-happy youngsters, like Frank and Jesse James, drifted from the ranks of the Rebel army into the ranks of outlaws. Bandits stood a good chance of being hailed as heroes of the defeated Confederacy. Folks believed they were taking back with their six-shooters what Yankee scalawags and city slickers had stolen with their fountain pens.

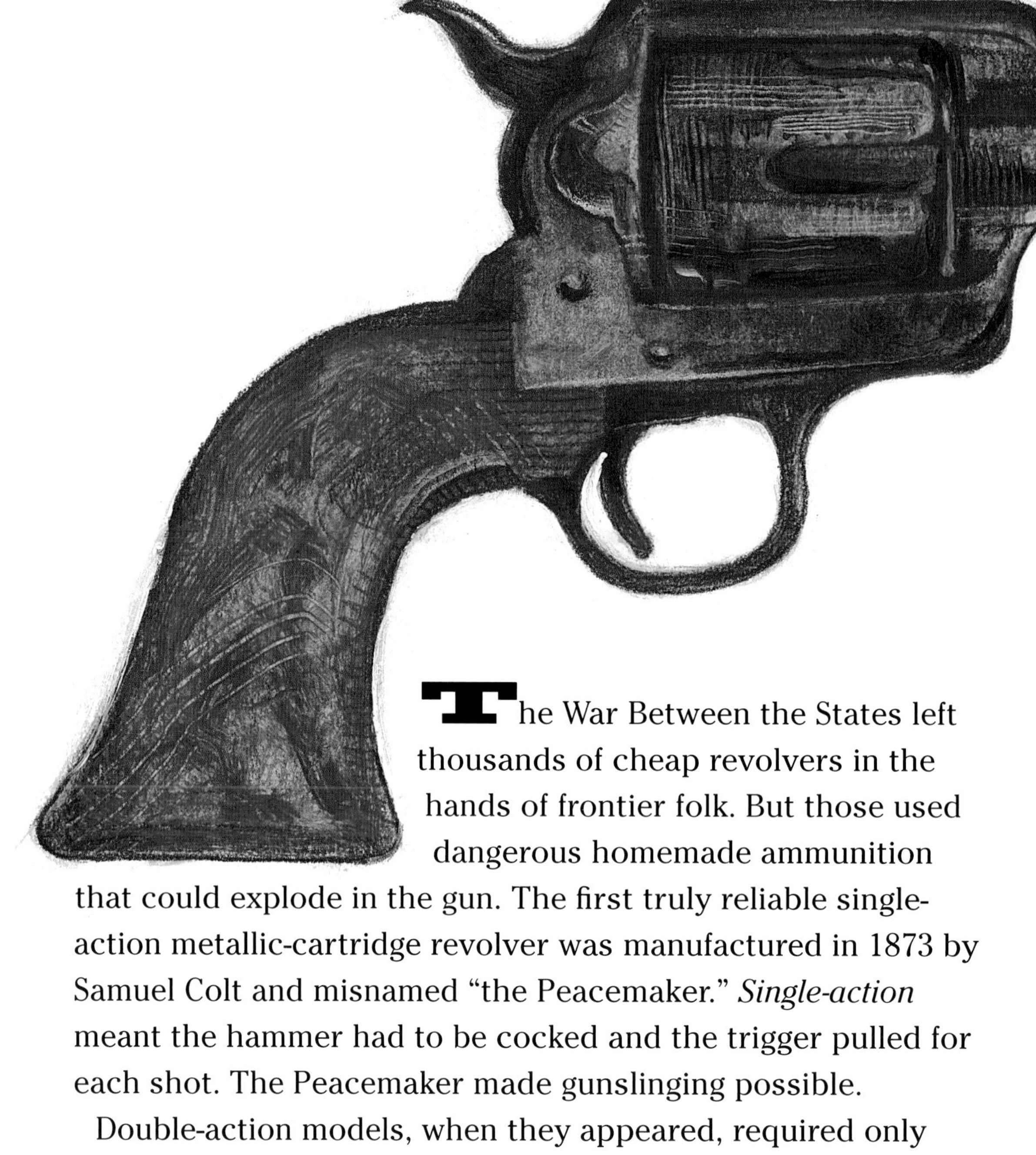

The War Between the States left thousands of cheap revolvers in the hands of frontier folk. But those used dangerous homemade ammunition that could explode in the gun. The first truly reliable single-action metallic-cartridge revolver was manufactured in 1873 by Samuel Colt and misnamed "the Peacemaker." *Single-action* meant the hammer had to be cocked and the trigger pulled for each shot. The Peacemaker made gunslinging possible.

Double-action models, when they appeared, required only pulling the trigger, but most gunslingers remained loyal to the Peacemaker. It was commonly said, "God made some men big and some small, but Colonel Colt made them equal all." Unlikely Western heroes like Six-Toed Pete, Three-Fingered Jack, Shotgun Collins, Blackjack Bill, Cold Chuck Johnny,

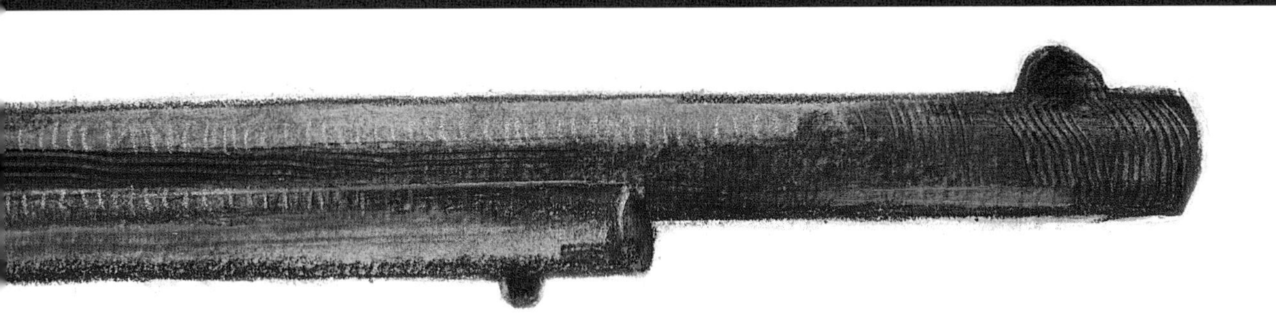

Dynamite Sam, Dark Alley Jim, Cockeyed Frank, and Turkey Creek Jack Johnson would never have become notorious outlaws without the help of Colonel Colt's equalizer.

The heroic gunslinger stories of fast-draw justice that spread out of the West grew mostly from clumsy murders committed by men carrying six-shooters stuffed awkwardly into their britches or holstered in a gunbelt. By the late 1880s gunfighters had pretty nearly killed one another off, but by then the tall tales of the Wild West had become legends firmly planted in the American imagination.

Wild Bill Hickok

The Legendary Gunfighter

If there was ever truly a gallant gunfighter, brave and handsome, who stood alone in the dusty street protecting honest citizens from black-hearted desperados, it surely was Wild Bill Hickok.

James Butler Hickok was born May 27, 1837, on a farm in La Salle County, Illinois. His biographer later wrote, "Fear was simply a quality he lacked." Young James set out to be a Western hero. He had what it took—a natural talent for shooting and storytelling.

During the Civil War he built a reputation for recklessness as a wagon master, scout, and spy. Bill claimed he rode his horse, Black Nellie, breakneck right through Confederate lines under heavy fire, leaping a twenty-foot gorge, just to show the Rebs what Union soldiers were made of. Black Nellie was his best friend, and he said she was smarter than a judge. By the end of the war he was known as Wild Bill.

After the war Wild Bill settled down to professional gambling. It was a dangerous and uncertain way to make a living, since most gamblers carried a tiny gun called a derringer, their "ace in the hole," used to shoot anyone suspected of having an ace up their sleeve.

One afternoon in the public square of Springfield, Missouri, Wild Bill faced a gunslinging cardsharp named Dave Tutt, with whom he'd had a disagreement. Their eyes narrowed, and they strode into the open until they stood some distance apart. Bill knew that Tutt's cousins were behind him in the crowd. Tutt went for his gun, but before he could even take aim, Wild Bill drew and fired, shattering the stillness. Wild Bill wheeled to confront Tutt's cousins. Their guns were already drawn. "Aren't you satisfied, gentlemen?" he asked, cool as an alligator. "Put up your shootin' irons!" And they did, all agreeing it had been a fair fight. *Harper's New Monthly Magazine* printed that story, with illustrations, in 1867. A reporter asked a witness, "Whatever happened to Dave Tutt?"

"Wild Bill never shoots twice at the same man," was the

answer. The legend of Wild Bill Hickok took off across the country like a Pony Express rider.

Wild Bill cut a grand figure, tall and handsome, the best-looking man west of the Mississippi, with flowing auburn hair and blue eyes. He was a legend in his own time. Folks in Abilene were looking for just such a legendary gunfighter to maintain law and order in their prosperous cow town, where hundreds of rambunctious cowboys crowded the saloons. So they hired Wild Bill as their sheriff.

Wild Bill could end a fracas just by scowling at the rowdy cowboys from under his eyebrows like a mean old bull. He disdained the Peacemaker and wore two ivory-handled .36-caliber Colt Navy revolvers, butts forward, preferring the plainsman's underhand draw, sometimes called "the twist." Bill offered troublemakers a choice between the train out of town and the cemetery in the morning. Even notorious gunslingers like John Wesley Hardin chose the train. Hickok was widely known to be the best pistol shot of all time, and he slept with his guns on. But he was quick to point out that a gunfighter's survival depended not on how well he shot, but on how well he shot back.

By December of 1871 folks in Abilene decided they'd had enough of cowboys and gunplay. The city council told the drovers to take their cattle and boisterous cowboys somewhere else. And they suggested to Wild Bill, after he shot his own deputy by mistake, that he might move along, too.

Bill went back to gambling full-time and started drinking. He drifted through Kansas City, Topeka, and Springfield, leaving behind a trail of bodies and tall tales. In Solomon, Kansas, trapped between a murderer behind him and one in front of him, he drew his ivory-handled revolvers and shot in two directions at once, killing them both. He stood up to fifty armed Texans at the Kansas City Fair just to prevent the band from playing "Dixie."

He even outlived a newspaper report of his own death and accused dime novel writer Ned Buntline of trying to murder him with a pen.

In 1873 Bill joined Buffalo Bill's Wild West Show, but he soon left, blaming his failing eyesight on the stage lights. He married Agnes Lake Thatcher but couldn't settle down and returned alone to the West, wearing glasses with smoked lenses.

In all his long experience as a gunslinger and lawman, Wild Bill had always claimed the seat in the corner when playing cards, so that no plug-ugly could get the drop on him. But on the afternoon of August 2, 1876, he tempted fate, sitting down to play poker with his back to an open door, and a cross-eyed saddle tramp named Jack McCall shot him from behind. McCall claimed Wild Bill had killed his brother, but

most thought he just wanted to be the man who shot Wild Bill Hickok. According to legend, Wild Bill was holding two pair, aces and eights, a hand known ever after as "the dead man's hand."

Before they hanged his murderer, someone asked why he'd shot Wild Bill in the back instead of meeting him face-to-face. McCall answered, "I wasn't looking to commit suicide."

Calamity Jane

The Heroine of the Plains

The wildest woman in the Wild West could tell a whopper that would make a mule skinner blush. Calamity couldn't abide watching the boys ride off without her to look for adventure, especially since she could outshoot them, outride them, and outwork them, too, if it came to that. So she swapped her skirts for a pair of britches, strapped on a six-shooter, and rode off through the badlands to dig for gold and drink red-eye whiskey with the boys in the goldfields.

Martha Jane Cannary was born in Mercer County, Missouri—in 1844, according to the census, or 1852, as she claimed. She learned to shoot and ride as a little girl traveling with her family on the long, dangerous trail to Virginia City, Montana.

In 1874, dressed in men's work clothes, she joined a railroad construction crew. Later she passed herself off as a boy so that she could hire on with the army, hauling supplies out of Fort Laramie. When she was caught skinny-dipping with her pals in Hat Creek, the scandalized officer in charge told her to pull her britches on and get out. But General Crook needed a first-class scout for his campaign against the Sioux, so he rehired Martha Jane.

Folks said she got named Calamity because she was a calamity to any man who crossed her. In Dodge City she set some poor galoot to dancing with rapid fire from her six-shooter because he'd been fool enough to make wisecracks concerning the condition of her undergarments. Brawling landed her in jail in Cheyenne in 1876. Calamity Jane was never an outlaw, but drinking and picking fights got her into trouble and made her famous.

She fell in love with Wild Bill Hickok in Deadwood. Both were dime-novel legends, and both could spin a good yarn for gullible Eastern newspapermen. Calamity claimed she'd panned for gold in the goldfields and ridden hell-bent for leather as a Pony Express rider through the toughest stretch in the Black Hills country. Bandits and Indians stayed clear, she said, because they feared her reputation as a crack shot.

Calamity claimed she'd rescued the Deadwood stage and saved the precious mail and the lives of six passengers from marauding Indians by leaping into the driver's seat from her horse and grabbing the reins. She claimed to have been Wild Bill Hickok's wife, too, but there is no record of a genuine romance. Her larger-than-life legend had her nearly splitting Jack McCall's head with a meat cleaver after he murdered Hickok. This, like many of Calamity's stories, simply wasn't so.

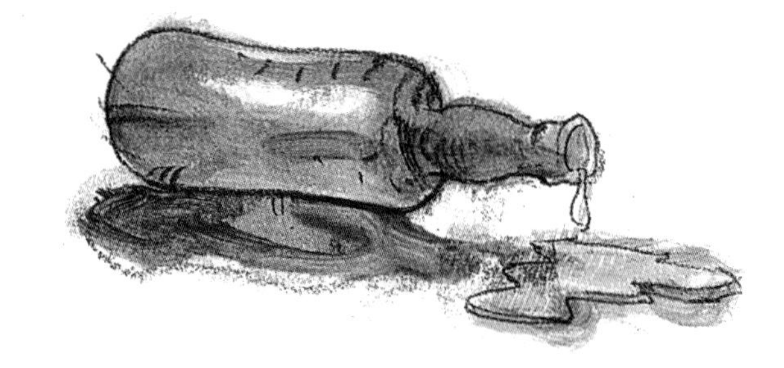

But Calamity Jane stood her ground with the town doctor when the dreaded smallpox broke out in Deadwood in 1878. She nursed a dying girl, a wounded man, and a sick baby. But the public wasn't so interested in that true story of her courage.

As she got older, Calamity lived by making appearances in dime museums and hawking a cheap pamphlet containing her memoirs. She died in 1903 near Deadwood, and her last wish was to be buried next to Wild Bill Hickok. Her friends managed to bury her twenty feet from his grave. They even changed the date of her death on her tombstone to coincide with the twenty-seventh anniversary of Wild Bill's murder.

Doc Holliday

The Lone Gunman

Of all the dark and desperate men, none was quite like Doc Holliday. Skeletal and racked by a killing, tubercular cough, he drifted from cow town to mining camp living on rotgut whiskey and raw nerve. He was deadly as a steely-eyed viper, dangerous as a wounded wolf, and by all accounts a pretty good dentist.

John Holliday was born in Valdosta, Georgia, in 1852 into an aristocratic Southern family, or so he said. It's certain that he studied dentistry in Baltimore. At twenty he was living a quiet, respectable life in Atlanta when he began to cough up blood. Diagnosed with advanced consumption (tuberculosis), the young dentist knew he would soon waste away.

Doc's only hope to cheat fate for a while was to breathe the dry air of the Southwest. So he moved to Texas, where the odds favored a quick and violent death. There he might die with his boots on, instead of "coughing his guts out" in a hospital bed. He studied the tricks of professional card players, and since he was frail and sickly, he took to practicing diligently with his new Colt Peacemaker. It wasn't long until Wyatt Earp claimed, "Doc Holliday was the most skillful gambler and the deadliest man with a six-gun I ever knew." Earp called him a gentleman, almost a poet, but dangerous!

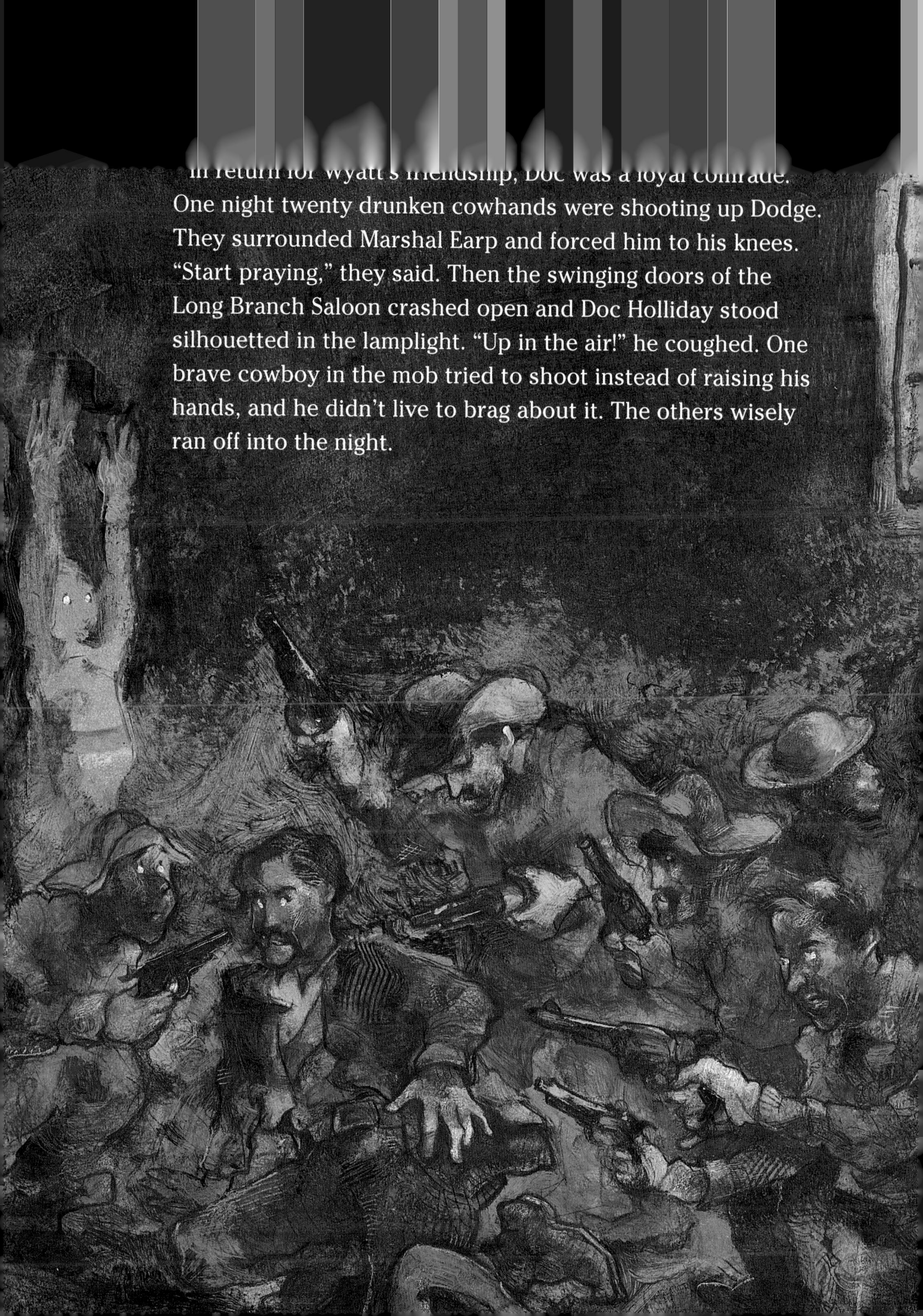

In return for Wyatt's friendship, Doc was a loyal comrade. One night twenty drunken cowhands were shooting up Dodge. They surrounded Marshal Earp and forced him to his knees. "Start praying," they said. Then the swinging doors of the Long Branch Saloon crashed open and Doc Holliday stood silhouetted in the lamplight. "Up in the air!" he coughed. One brave cowboy in the mob tried to shoot instead of raising his hands, and he didn't live to brag about it. The others wisely ran off into the night.

SALOON

Doc called whiskey his medicine and prescribed it for himself in large doses. But he could still be deadly. When two thugs got the drop on him late at night, leveling their six-guns at his heart, Doc drew faster than a snake's tongue and shot them both before they could squeeze the triggers. Like many of Doc Holliday's victims, they died with surprised looks on their faces.

Some bad guys took to a life of violence through misfortune, or so they claimed, and some learned their murderous ways from the War Between the States. But "lead poisoning" was Doc Holliday's chosen way to die. In his search for a gunfighter's death, he killed some thirty men. But Doc never attempted to immortalize himself in dime novels.

By 1883 Doc was a skeletal vagabond. His drifting finally brought him to a sanitarium in Glenwood Springs, Colorado, where he died on November 8, 1887. The lone wolf who hoped only for a violent death died after all in the way he most feared—quietly, in a clean bed, with his boots off. His last words to the nurse were "This is funny."

Gunfight at the O.K. Corral

On October 26, 1881, in the silver-mining town of Tombstone, Arizona, the Earps met the Clantons in the most famous shoot-out of the Wild West. Virgil Earp was Tombstone's marshal, and Wyatt was his assistant. The Clantons were cowboys who thought the Earps were challenging the freedom of the open range. Trouble came when Virgil arrested the Clantons for stealing army mules. To get even, the Clantons said Doc Holliday had murdered a stage driver during a holdup planned by the Earps. Billy Clanton tried to make peace, but it was too late. Virgil, Wyatt, and Morgan Earp, along with Doc Holliday, strode down Fremont Street in their long coats. The Clantons and the McLaurys lined up against a wall in a scrubby vacant lot. They faced off not more than six feet apart.

Someone pulled the hammer back on a six-shooter. Doc Holliday and Morgan Earp opened fire. Thirty seconds later Billy Clanton, Frank McLaury, and Tom McLaury lay dead. Virgil, Morgan, and Doc were wounded.

The horrified citizens of Tombstone threatened to lynch all the Earps if they did any more killing.

Jesse James

America's Robin Hood

No outlaws caught the American imagination like the defiant brothers Jesse and Frank James. Beginning as Confederate irregulars in the War Between the States, the James gang rode on to become the most famous six-gun heroes of their day. They were admired by Missouri folks who needed to believe that someone could stand up to the Yankee bankers and railroad bosses. Somehow they held on to the belief that the South hadn't truly lost the war until Jesse James was shot in the back.

Before the war, slave-owning Missourians tried to force their neighbors in Kansas to become slave owners, too. Kansas abolitionists resisted, sometimes violently. For trigger-happy youngsters like the James brothers, revenge raids along the Kansas-Missouri border were a way of life. When the Civil War finally broke out, Frank James joined up with Quantrill's murderous Confederate irregulars, called bushwhackers. And after seeing his stepfather tortured and taking a beating himself from Union soldiers, Frank's little brother, Jesse, joined up, too. By the end of the war western Missouri was so devastated by guerrilla fighting that it was called "the burnt district."

Most defeated Rebels went home to rebuild their farms. But the James boys took the outlaw path. On February 13, 1866, they committed the first daylight bank robbery in the United States. The gang got away with $60,000. And if they needed more reason to avoid hard work, they found it in the admiration they received from newspapers and embittered Missouri farmers.

Eastern bankers hired the Pinkerton detective agency to track them down, but the law couldn't touch the James gang. Jesse became the champion of the defeated South. According to popular legend, Jesse paid off mortgages so that poor widows wouldn't lose their little farms to the hated Yankee bankers. Anyone suggesting that they'd never actually seen him do any such thing might well wind up dead in a ravine, like the Pinkerton detectives who were shot and left by the side of the road.

In sixteen years the James gang held up eleven banks, seven trains, three stagecoaches, one county fair, and one payroll messenger, and murdered at least sixteen clerks, tellers, and railroad workers. Between jobs Jesse sang in the choir at the Kearny Baptist Church. Soon every unsolved crime in the territory was blamed on the James gang, and by 1874 Jesse James seemed to be a one-man crime wave.

In January of 1875 Pinkerton agents surrounded the James family farm and tossed a flare through the window. It exploded, killing Jesse's nine-year-old half brother and injuring his mother, Zarelda. The raid reunited Missourians in their admiration for the outlaw and their hatred of

Yankees. At the same time, the first of many dime novels appeared that romanticized the exploits of the James gang.

But some citizens were not convinced. When the James gang rode into Northfield, Minnesota, intent on robbing the First National Bank, the townspeople met them with guns and rocks. Two of the outlaws fell dead in the street, and the rest hightailed it empty-handed.

Jesse and Frank continued robbing trains, reportedly more brutal and murderous than ever. In 1881 the governor put a price on Jesse's head: $10,000, dead or alive. Jesse hid out for a while in Belle Starr's place at Younger's Bend in Oklahoma, near the Canadian River.

Finally, disguised as Thomas Howard, a horse trader, Jesse moved with his wife and two children to a respectable little clapboard house in St. Joseph, Missouri. On April 3, 1882, Jesse, who rarely took his revolvers off, set them aside and climbed up on a chair to dust a picture in his sitting room. A new gang member named Bob Ford saw his chance to claim the reward and shot Jesse in the back of the head. He was known forever after as "the dirty little coward that shot Mr. Howard." Feelings ran so hot at the news of Jesse's murder that when a Missouri state official proclaimed his satisfaction at hearing of the outlaw's death, his fellow legislators threw their spittoons at him.

Jesse's mother supported herself by charging a quarter to view Jesse's grave on the family farm. Still, many people believed he had in fact faked his own death and disappeared. The flood of books praising Jesse's outlaw life was blamed for inspiring a juvenile crime wave in Eastern cities, and mailmen refused to deliver them.

Belle Starr

The Bandit Queen

Belle Starr loved handsome rustlers and fancy feathered hats and six-shooters. Her horse thieves didn't have to be clever or gallant or brave, but she liked them young and ready to ride. The boys all knew who ran the show, and Belle protected them as best she could from being lynched by angry ranchers or becoming the guest of honor at a policemen's hemp dance.

Myra Belle Shirley was born in 1848 near Carthage, Missouri. Her first love was good-looking, quarrelsome Cole Younger, who rode with her big brother Ed and the James boys, making life miserable for folk on the Kansas-Missouri border. By the end of the Civil War most of western Missouri, including her father's hotel, had been burned to the ground. Soon the family was "gone to Texas."

Belle settled down with a horse thief, bank robber, and murderer named Jim Reed. They had two children, but Jim got himself killed resisting arrest, so Myra Belle set up shop on her own, selling stolen livestock out of a crooked livery stable.

She married Sam Starr and became known as Belle Starr. Belle led a gang of horse thieves and rustlers from her hideout on the Canadian River, which she called Younger's Bend. Accounts of her exploits in the press soon made Belle Starr everybody's favorite criminal.

She liked to ride into Fort Smith dressed in a wide-brimmed hat trimmed with feathers and bangles to play the piano in the saloon.

Belle was finally caught red-handed stealing horses and spent nine months in prison. When she was released, she returned to the safety of Younger's Bend and invited all her new jailhouse friends to come live with her there. "I am a friend to any brave and gallant outlaw," she proclaimed.

When her husband, Sam, got shot in a disagreement with a policeman, Belle found a handsome new boyfriend known as Blue Duck. Before long, young Blue was facing the hangman's noose—he'd gotten liquored up and murdered a farmer. Belle hired a lawyer and sent him to Washington, D.C., to persuade President Grover Cleveland to spare young Blue's life. She won his life, but not his freedom.

Belle's son, Ed, was soon old enough to steal horses on his own. When he got caught, Belle sent her lawyer back to Washington. This time she won a full pardon. Belle's charm and notoriety had not diminished with the years, but in 1889 she was bushwhacked while riding the lonely road to Younger's Bend. The murder was generally blamed on her newest husband, Jim July, though he was never arrested. Her son, Ed, was also suspected.

Belle was laid to rest at Younger's Bend. Her tombstone is inscribed with a bell and a star and a horse. The inscription reads:

Shed not for her the bitter tear
Nor give the heart to vain regret
'Tis but the casket that lies here
The gem that filled it sparkles yet.

Billy the Kid

America's Rosy-Cheeked Desperado

Billy the Kid was a freedom-loving boy who set off to find adventure or gold . . . or violent death. But Billy always said, "What's the use of looking on the gloomy side of everything?"

Henry McCarty was born on November 23, 1859, or thereabouts, in an Irish slum of New York City. He was placed by the New York Children's Aid Society with a farmer named William Antrim, who took a shine to Henry's mother, Catherine. After the Civil War, Antrim took them west, and in 1873 he married Catherine. They settled in Silver City, New Mexico, and the boy happily took his stepfather's name, William.

His teacher recalled William as a scrawny fellow with delicate hands and an artistic nature. William helped with chores after school and loved reading gunfighter stories in the *Police Gazette*. Some called him a troublemaker, but his teacher said he was no worse than other boys growing up in a mining camp.

Billy's mother died of consumption in 1874. He was only fourteen when he went to work at the Silver City hotel. According to the manager, William was the first boy hired on there who never stole anything. But some older boys talked him into hiding clothes they'd stolen from a Chinese laundry just for a laugh, and a policeman thought locking William up for a few days would teach him a lesson. Instead, the frightened boy wriggled up the chimney and hightailed it across the territorial line.

In 1877 Billy turned up at the Camp Grant army post in Arizona, a six-gun tucked into his britches. He liked his job hauling logs except for the ribbing he took from the camp blacksmith, an oversized bully named Windy Cahill. "You're just as pretty as a girl. Ain't ya?" Windy taunted. One day Billy drew his six-gun and shot his tormentor.

One witness said, "He had no choice but to use his equalizer." But Windy hadn't even had a gun.

This time when Billy escaped from the guardhouse, he changed his name to William H. Bonney. He was a desperado on the run when he hired on as a cattle guard for John Tunstall, a young English cattleman. The kid gunslinger, still hoping for a fresh start, had unknowingly joined the cattlemen's side in the Lincoln County War. The ranchers, who had carved out cattle empires on the prairie, were at war with the merchants in town. Both sides wanted profitable government contracts to supply military posts and Indian reservations with beef and livestock. The merchant side bribed local lawmen and hired a gunfighter named Morton to murder Billy's boss and new friend, John Tunstall.

When Billy tried bringing in the gunman himself, the crooked sheriff of Lincoln County laughed and tossed the Kid in jail. After a few days the sheriff released Billy without his rifle. Billy the Kid wanted deadly revenge. He shot Morton and one of his men after they had surrendered.

On April Fools' Day in 1878 Billy killed the sheriff and took back his rifle. Before he was through in Lincoln County, he'd led a shoot-out that lasted five days in the streets of Lincoln. It ended when the leader of the cattlemen was killed. Billy

escaped and took up with a ragtag gang of ordinary horse thieves, stealing from the ranchers and from the Apaches on the reservation.

The governor of New Mexico, Lew Wallace, promised even then to pardon the Kid if he would testify against the men responsible for killing John Tunstall. So Billy gave himself up, saying he had no wish to fight anymore. But the governor was too busy writing his book *Ben Hur* to keep a watchful eye on the proceedings. Billy, fearing a double cross, slipped his small hands out of the handcuffs and went back to horse thieving.

Stealing horses was considered even worse than murder. Horse thieves were shot on the spot or hanged from the nearest tree. Local ranchers elected Pat Garrett, a friend of Billy's, to hunt him down. Garrett's posse finally surrounded the outlaws at a house near Stinking Springs and cut off their food supply until they had to surrender. Billy was quickly convicted of murder and sentenced to hang. Again the Kid slipped from his handcuffs, this time while being escorted to the outhouse. He killed two deputies and escaped.

Billy lived on his own in the hills after that, showing up to dance at fiestas and disappearing like a ghost, with the law always close on his heels. On July 14, 1881, Billy and Sheriff Garrett ran into each other again. Billy, just returned from a dance, was wandering about in search of a midnight snack. Billy saw a shadow. "*¿Quién es?* Who is it?" he asked. Garrett recognized the Kid's voice. He drew his gun and fired twice, shooting Henry McCarty—alias William Antrim, alias William H. Bonney, alias Billy the Kid—dead.

Eight novels appeared within a year claiming to tell the true story of Billy the Kid, though there wasn't much truth in any of them. Pat Garrett himself wrote a book, inspired, he said, "by an impulse to correct the thousands of false statements." But from that very book, a bestseller, come some of the biggest lies.

Some claimed that Billy the Kid killed a man for each of his twenty-one years. In another story, the gun used to kill Billy was the same one worn by Wild Bill Hickok when he was murdered in Deadwood. Some even believed Billy was still alive in 1920, going by the name Walk-along Smith.

Joaquin Murietta

THE GHOST OF SONORA

The most elusive desperado ever pursued by a posse was just a fable woven from stories of stolen gold and dreams of revenge. But Joaquin haunted the sleep of the greedy gringos who'd stolen the land and all its gold, because the Ghost of Sonora vowed to pay them back in blood.

In the early 1850s, laws were passed in California to keep Mexicans from working in the goldfields and to drive them from their land. Bitter resentment and poverty made hit-and-run outlaws of some Mexicans. In the night around campfires, wishful Spanish-speaking storytellers blended the real-life bad guys together into one handsome desperado named Joaquin.

Tales of a ruthless Spanish gentleman, sworn to kill gringos, reached the ears of nervous stagecoach passengers and saloon keepers and spread to the offices of worried profiteers and politicians. Fear of the elusive Joaquin grew with every robbery and murder. In 1853 the governor offered a reward of $1,500 for any bandit named Joaquin, dead or alive. A Texas Ranger named Harry Love organized a band of bounty hunters to comb the countryside, determined to kill someone. Honest men named Joaquin fearfully began changing their names.

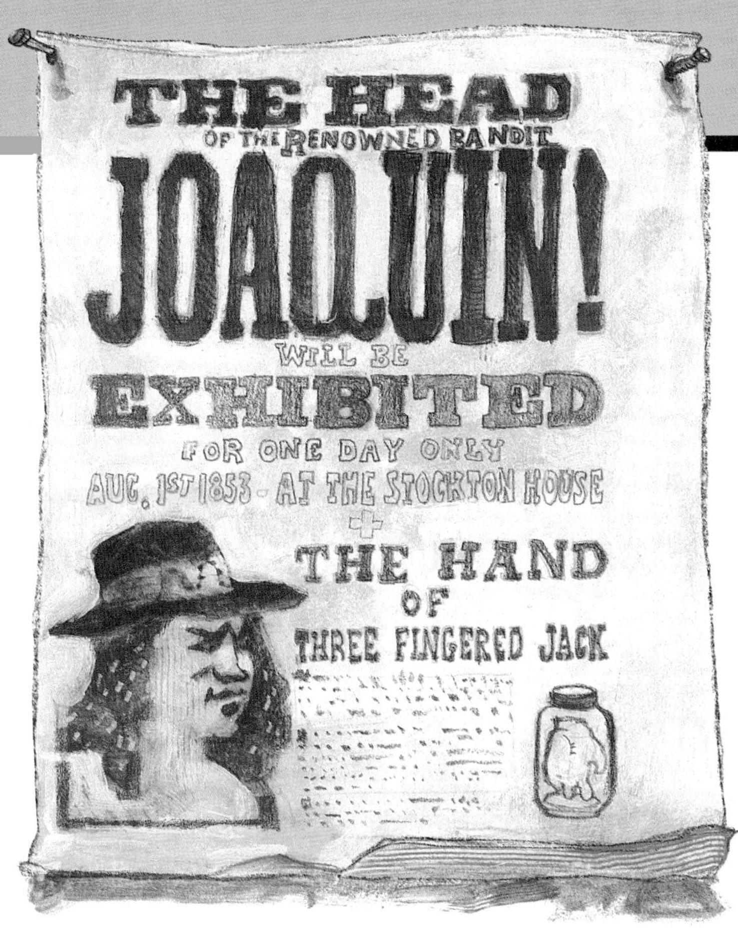

Two months later Love's Rangers shot it out with a band of Mexican outlaws eating in the Arroyo Cantina. When the smoke cleared, two Mexicans were dead. One was Manuel Garcia, also known as Three-Fingered Jack, who was wanted for murder. The rangers cut his three-fingered hand off and dropped it in a jar of alcohol. Since the reward was for Joaquin, the rangers put the other man's head in a jar. After all, how could anyone know what Joaquin looked like, since he didn't really exist? They collected the reward, plus a $5,000 bonus from grateful government officials.

At least one San Francisco paper called the whole story a humbug, but early historians accepted Joaquin Murietta as a real person. The head and hand were displayed for years around California, attracting large audiences. They finally landed in Jordan's Museum of Medical Oddities, jars number 563 and 564.

Black Bart

"Reach for the Sky!"

In 1877 an elderly gentleman who'd worked hard all his life felt inspired to take up robbing stagecoaches.

Charles Bolton was an honest farmer, soldier, and prospector. He'd never been a success, but he still figured he deserved comfort and respectability in his old age. Inspired by stories of heroic outlaws, he made a black hood from a flour sack and became the mysterious Black Bart, scourge of Wells Fargo stagecoaches. He planned each robbery carefully, studying every narrow pass and jutting rock near the Russian River in California. He knew exactly when to step out from behind a boulder and block the road. Leveling his double-barreled shotgun at the driver, Black Bart commanded, "Throw down the box!"

His gang backed him up from behind rocks and trees. No armed guard dared challenge him. But in his entire career as a highwayman, Black Bart never fired a single shot. After emptying the strongbox, he slipped away on foot, leaving behind only a poem signed "the po 8."

There were never any tracks for a posse to follow, since he never actually rode a horse. In spite of the Wells Fargo Company's $800 reward, Black Bart went on for six years before slipping up on his twenty-eighth holdup. In 1883 he was finally tracked down by a determined detective on foot.

J. B. Hume took a linen handkerchief found at the scene of a robbery to all ninety-one Chinese laundries in San Francisco, finally identifying the owner by its laundry mark. He found Mr. Bolton, a dapper gentleman with a fancy walking stick, living comfortably in a small hotel. Mr. Bolton's gang turned out to be painted broomsticks, propped up behind trees and rocks. Mr. Bolton went quietly. He was tried and convicted and ended up in San Quentin Prison.

Here I lay me down to sleep
To wait the coming morrow.
Perhaps success, perhaps defeat,
And everlasting sorrow.
But come what may I'll try it on,
My condition can't be worse,
If there's money in that box,
'Tis money in my purse.

—BLACK BART
the po 8

BOSTON PUBLIC LIBRARY
3 9999 03550 186 3